THE STORY OF THE SEASHORE

John S. Goodall

Margaret K. McElderry Books
New York

Copyright © 1990 by John S. Goodall

Margaret K. McElderry Books
Macmillan Publishing Company
866 Third Avenue
New York, NY 10022

Printed in Hong Kong
First United States Edition
10 9 8 7 6 5 4 3 2 1

Library of Congress Cataloging-in-Publication Data
Goodall, John S.
   The story of the seashore/John S. Goodall.—1st American ed.
        p.   cm.
   Summary: Traces the changing scene at the beach through various
eras from bath houses, bathing costumes, and donkey rides to wind
and body surfing, wind sailing, and other modern amusements.
Features half pages that reveal hidden portions of the illustrations.
   1. Seashore—Recreational use—Juvenile literature. 2. Toy and
movable books—Specimens.   [1. Beaches—Pictorial works.
2. Seashore—Pictorial works.   3. Toy and movable books.]
I. Title.
GV191.62.G66 1990 796.5′3—dc20
89–8328 CIP AC
ISBN 0–689–50491–8

In the early 1800s King George III took his family to Weymouth for their health, and so began a fashion for seashore holidays and the development of the seaside town as a place in which to enjoy yourself, whatever the weather.

7

11

19

TOYS

HIGH
STREET

27

31

51